THE BETTER BETTY

CHEURLIE PIERRE-RUSSELL

BOOKS BY C. PIERRE-RUSSELL:

Little Kitty Goes to School

Sheila the Shy Shark

Broken before the Storm

The Beauty of Love in Those we Shame

Save the Missing Penny

*Making Dollars Make $ense:
Business Ownership at any Age*

Butter Me Fly: My Way Home

The Special Little Sister

The Better Betty

Friendly Monsters: Behind the Computer

TABLE OF CONTENTS

Chapter 1: Monday, Monday 1

Chapter 2: Betty's World 19

Chapter 3: Little Lies 25

Chapter 4: Aftermath 43

Chapter 5: Final Call 50

Chapter 6: Betty's Beginning 66

Epilogue 73

Summary 77

About the Author 78

CHAPTER 1
MONDAY, MONDAY

A nd so, it was Monday morning again; that stupid, horrible day seemed to come around once a week—whoever would have thought it? And as was usual on Monday mornings, it was dark, gloomy and grim outside, enormous raindrops sliding down the all the houses' windowpanes and splattering on the paths and sidewalks. Great big brown muddy puddles covered the streets, and all the trees' and plants' leaves hung heavy with all the wetness, looking sad and miserable, as if they, too, really hated Mondays.

The lamplights were still lit, and the birds only just starting to sing.

It felt like the middle of the night.

But inside all the houses on the gloomy, sodden street, the kitchen windows were all aglow and the curtains were beginning to be pulled back.

You see, not everyone hated Mondays! Not at all! As weird as this may sound, in some of these homes, kids were eagerly getting ready for school—and bizarrely, they even liked the idea. Yes, middle-school kids all over the town were now launching themselves out of their beds with tired but smiling faces, showering, brushing their pearly white teeth and preparing for another great school day, their school bags full to bursting with books and pens and sports gear.

And so it was that on this Monday morning, in house number 13, Cherry Avenue. This address was where Misha and George—twin brother and sister, aged thirteen—were seated at their kitchen table loudly clattering their spoons in their great big bowls of cereal.

George pushed his breakfast around the bowl as his mother looked on.

"Enjoying that, Georgie?" his mother asked. It pulled George back to reality. George nodded, suddenly realizing the food was actually supposed to go in his mouth. It seemed he was 'away with the fairies' again, as his mother called it—daydreaming, in other words.

George was already thinking about sport, his favorite lesson which would be coming along right at the end of his day. And he just couldn't wait!

George's sister—younger by a whole minute—sat at the table too, twiddling with some colored threads. "What are you doing?" George asked, wrinkling his nose. "That doesn't look like breakfast."

"Thread. It's *thread*, you idiot," she said, smiling broadly. "I do sewing. After school. I'm doing a cat thing. You know, like embroidery. Kitty, with whiskers."

"A cat thing? A kitty? Sounds…a-ma-zing!" He grinned and rolled his eyes as if it was a boring concept. "Anyway, why would anyone with even half a brain stay behind after school? You've got a whole day of boring lessons and you're stupid enough to stay behind and do more! Only a *moron* would do that…"

But he wasn't serious. He was just poking fun at his sister. He really loved how creative and clever she was, while he was sportier and athletic, and in secret, just a little bit brainier. Not a lot, but just about enough to make a claim that he was the clever one.

But together, if you added everything up, the range of subjects these two kids loved were right off the scale! They loved just about every class and soaked up all their homework like sponges, always keen to learn and outdo each other.

Their parents were so proud, and rightly so!

Both these kids wanted to go to university in a few years.

They took after their parents. Their mom was a physician in the town hospital and their father was an accountant. Both those jobs needed at least a little bit of brain, so said their dad. And it looked like both the kids were following right in their footsteps.

Then there was the other teen in the house on the other side of number 13, at house number 15! Wow, she was a brainy one as well!

That child had a shock of red frizzy hair and freckles all over her pale face, and she was called Miriam.

Miriam was a brainbox—everyone said so, and she went to the same school and was in the same class as George and Misha. This girl's parents had moved over from some far-flung country called England in the United Kingdom—at least a million miles across the ocean, a strange and mysterious place where they all ate mashed potato and pies, and fish and chips.

It sounded like a strange country, but Miriam was not strange at all. She was just clever. Miriam was always top of her class in all her own subjects.

Boy, all these kids were intelligent.

And most of all, every one of them love, love, loved school!

The clock hands ticked around the huge white clock face and edged toward 07:30. In house number 13, the twins Misha and George jumped up from their seats and grabbed a hold of their bags enthusiastically.

"Time to go!" George said, shovelling the last spoonful of cereal in his mouth while his sister pulled a small plastic box from her school bag and pushed the colored threads and needles into it, before snapping it shut and stuffing it back into the bag.

"George, are we going to knock on next door for Betty?" Misha said as she fastened her coat. Ah. Betty.

What to say about Betty…?

To be honest, the reason this story hasn't even mentioned Betty so far is because Betty was kind of—forgettable, to be truthful. Betty was forgettable—and not a bit like George, Misha or Miriam—because she didn't stand out at all. Not anymore.

And she didn't stand out because hardly anyone ever saw Betty. And when they did, they noticed Betty for all the wrong things, the bad things, the stupid things Betty did, things that got her into awful trouble.

Well, Betty was the girl at number 11, the house to the left of number 13 and one house removed from number 15 where Miriam lived.

Betty had started out as a good kid really, everyone had thought so, but it was fair to say that lately, she'd become a little bit—what was the word, now—well, a little bit lazy. Lazy, yes.

That was the only word for it. L-a-z-y. Lazy! Laaaaa-zeeee!

However, you spelled it, it still was a word that looked just like Betty. Poor Betty. Lazy Betty. When Betty stood in front of her tall bedroom mirror, she looked lazy from all sides. She now had a label attached, like a big neon sign pinned to her forehead. "Here comes lazy Betty," people would say. "Here she is, got out of bed for once. Unbelievable!"

And the teachers at the school would *tut* and frown when they spotted Betty while all the other kids giggled and hid behind their hands.

That *lazy* label meant Betty liked to sit on her chair and not move, not for hours at a time. Once, she'd sat in the same place on the couch for eighteen whole hours, until she finally was forced to get up for something to eat!

That was what people said, anyway.

Lazy meant Betty liked to say no when other kids her age was saying *yes,* or even *mmm, yes please,* to activities that might mean getting up off the sofa and moving from in front of the TV. Things like sports, and walking, and skiing, volleyball or even visiting the cinema or a museum—people said lazy, can't-be-bothered Betty would say no to them all. And usually, that was exactly what Betty did, so she lived up to her label and never disappointed anyone.

And *lazy* meant Betty had no idea of anything she would like to do—either at school, after school, or in the future. If anyone asked her, she would just shrug and say, "Don't care really," or "Look, shut up and don't ask stupid questions."

Betty, it seemed, had lost her way.

Unlike the other kids of her age, Betty hated school, loathed it, detested it, and as far as she was concerned, school was repulsive; it stank.

Oh, yes, that ugly l-word—lazy—had burrowed its way right into Betty's soul, just like a beetle deep inside a dung heap. And it looked like the l-word had found itself some cozy spot to nestle in and refused to come out.

This had turned Betty into perhaps the laziest teen this street had ever accommodated! And along with the laziness, Betty was putting on weight, her skin was turning greasy and sallow, and her hair was limp and lifeless.

But being lazy is not exactly a crime, is it?

There are so many reasons to be lazy, including health problems.

But unfortunately, Betty had none of these valid reasons for being lazy. She was also turning into other forms of a teen monster. She was spending hours chatting to boys on Facebook—boys she didn't really know. Older boys.

She'd gone out and pretended to be older than she was, covered in makeup and with a fake piercing in her nose, just so she could get a tattoo in secret, on the back of her shoulder! Mom and Dad still did not know it was even there.

And then, feeling even more of a teenage rebel, she had started ignoring Grandpa and Grandma when they bothered to visit her at home, preferring to sit in her bedroom wasting her time on social media, bad-mouthing the very people who had stood by her all these years. And she was rude and selfish.

"My mom is so fat, she can't fit through the doors anymore," she giggled as she wrote this to one girl. "And my dad, he's just stupid."

"Why stupid?" the girl asked.

"Because."

"Because what?"

"Well, for one thing, he leaves his wallet on the bedside table and then goes to sleep!" Betty said.

The girl was a bit confused.

"My dad does that too," she said. "I don't know what you mean."

"Let's just say I bought a tattoo," Betty said. "And it cost me $100!"

"I still don't know what you mean," Betty's friend said on Facebook chat. The girl sounded genuinely confused. Betty wondered just how stupid her 'friend' could possibly be.

"So, let's say I want something," Betty said. "I haven't got any money. But my dad's wallet is there and he's snoring his stupid head off…"

"You don't!"

"I do. I mean, what he doesn't know, right?"

The girl just didn't know what to write anymore but this attention elevated Betty to new heights of acting out. It was kinda ridiculous and strange, and only the sort of thing a loser would do. But it was also brave, and risky, and something the kids could look up to. Bad kids loved it all, bad kids just like Betty was becoming.

"Cool!" the girl typed.

And then the word started to go around: Betty was a thief. And from her own parents, too! How great was that? And she was only thirteen!

And sadly, these weren't the only ways in which Betty was acting out. You name it; if it was bad, Betty was starting to do it.

Sometimes, even the stench of cigarette smoke seeped out from under Betty's bedroom door late at night while her folks were sleeping.

Smoking was what all the cool kids did in secret, even ones younger than Betty; Betty knew she was such a cool kid now! And what made it even better was that her dad bought her the cigarettes—without even having a clue about it. The fact she had managed to take $100 in one single hit one night made her feel even bolder to try for something bigger next time.

Anyway, if Dad was so stupid as to keep that sort of money in loose notes in his wallet, he deserved everything he got, right?

***

And so we return to the question thirteen-year-old Misha had asked her brother George when they were on their way to school.

"Well, *will* we call next door for Betty, or not?"

George looked pensive for just a moment. Then he spoke.

"Last time we called next door for Betty," George said, "we got in trouble. Deep trouble. Because she walked so slooooooowly! Anyway, she didn't even want to go, did she?"

So, they decided to give lazy Betty a miss. And if she did want to go to school for a change, she was probably already at the bus stop. Well, she would be, wouldn't she? The last time she'd been late arriving at school—much later than the day on which she'd gone with Misha and George—she'd been called into the headmistress's room and given a terrible punishment of staying behind at school for a whole week, to do chores and write essays until she felt as if her eyes could almost fall out of her lazy, nothing-matters head.

So, everyone knew she wouldn't be late again. It was a no-brainer, they said; no kid would want to get punished that way again.

Oh. No, not Betty! Not late again! No way would she be late twice in a couple of weeks. If she wasn't careful, she could get expelled. That was surely enough to scare any child.

***

Misha and George hurried to the bus stop where they then stood awaiting the big yellow coach that would drive them into the school.

They always sat side by side on the bus, George with his headphones on, Misha with her nose buried in a book. Misha sure loved to read.

And on the days when lazy Betty decided to put in an appearance at school, Betty always sat behind them, blowing bubbles with her bubble gum and being generally irritating and annoying, probably on purpose.

Once, a nasty huge gum bubble got stuck in Misha's sleek black ponytail, and George had had to try and chew it out with his teeth. Another day, Misha was looking at her embroidery on the bus, leaning forward to look at her stitching up close when naughty Betty kicked the back of her seat, causing Misha's head to shoot forward—propelling the sewing needle right into Misha's chin!

That day, Misha ended up seeing the school nurse and she'd had to lie about how it'd happened, not wanting bad Betty to get into more trouble than she was always in anyway.

"The bus kind of…jolted," she'd said.

And then the poor bus driver had gotten into trouble for his erratic driving that had caused a girl to sustain a facial injury. Now, the drivers were all a little wary of Misha, thinking she was the girl who told tall tales that got them into trouble at work and threatened all the drivers' jobs.

The bus pulled in, and quite a few kids of around the same age got on. But someone was missing. The driver looked at George and Misha as they offered their bus fares to him, counting it out.

"So, where's your friend today, young man?" the usual driver said to George, eyeing Misha suspiciously from the corner of his eye.

"She's not with us, duh!" George said, cheekily.

"I can see that myself, young George, but why not?"

"Mister Morris," George said, so politely now, addressing the driver. "I think Betty's probably still in bed, you know? I mean, she's *lazy*. That's why we didn't call for her. Bone idle Betty, that's what I call her now," George said.

The bus driver just threw back his head and laughed, then nodded.

"A lazy young lady, is she? Well, best let her be, then. Let her be late and lazy and don't get involved. Kids like that only get themselves in more and more trouble. Stay away from a girl like that. And anyway," he said. "I've heard rumors about that girl. So, mark my words, kids, you're better off out of it."

The kids nodded but wondered what the rumors were, not daring to ask. George sucked on a lollipop while Misha pulled a book from her school bag, same as she always did. They sat in silence all the way to school, but Misha scanned the sidewalks for Betty just in case she was walking to school for a change. It was a wasted thought; Betty—young, acting-out, brainless Betty—had no intention of showing up for lessons.

They were all such a waste of her time.

CHAPTER 2
BETTY'S WORLD

B ack on the street where all the children lived, and deep inside the walls of number 11 where Betty resided, nothing stirred—nothing at all.

The kitchen table was bare. Nobody sat there eating breakfast and the dirty dishes were still piled in the sink from the night before, unwashed.

Mom and Dad were out at work already; they both believed in being up at the break of dawn and out on the road to work by seven o'clock.

On this Monday morning, they had happily left thirteen-year-old Betty back at home in bed; they trusted her to get off to school by herself. After all, she was a teen now, not a little child—so why would they not trust her to be by herself and to ensure she got off to school on time?

Betty's dad was a businessman with 'his fingers in many pies', so people said; people talked of him being an entrepreneur, a man who could make things happen. Big things. Important things.

Betty's mom was a personal assistant to a female celebrity blogger who was always on the television for something or other, and she had to work some very long days to keep her demanding client happy.

Mom imagined such great things for Betty too; these days, as she told Betty, a woman could be whatever she wanted as long as she worked hard, kept her eye on her goal and let nothing stand in her way.

And there was nothing at all to stand in Betty's way. Was there?

"So, what do you want to be, Betty?" Mom had recently asked her daughter.

"I'm going to be a scientist, Mom," Betty said. "So, I'll have to be late home from school quite a bit, because I'll do the after-school classes."

This was quite a different response from the one Betty gave her teachers or her classmates when they posed her the same question, when she would always say, "I don't care," or "Don't ask such stupid questions! Can I go now?"

The world Betty lived in at home was a world away from the truth.

The truth meant nothing to her. Nothing at all. The truth was a waste of time. Everyone knew that. You never got anywhere in life by telling the truth. White lies didn't matter. And actually, gray ones were okay too. And sometimes just downright filthy rotten lies—if they kept people quiet—were all okay too.

And believe me, Betty told them all—white, gray, and filthy lies had become quite a hobby for young Betty lately. And telling lies was something Betty excelled at. At least she was good at something.

Her mom hadn't thought any more about Betty's future; her Betty was a clever girl, a devoted girl, a truthful girl— who would do well for herself, and so she surely would have everything it took to become an excellent scientist.

Mom trusted all the words Betty spoke, even if her girl was quieter than she used to be and perhaps just turning a touch rebellious lately, with her use of black eyeliner and too-short skirts for a girl of thirteen.

Why didn't Mom worry? Well, because her Betty came in late most evenings and told her parents all about the extra tuition she was receiving after regular classes; she really made her parents' hearts swell with pride. And every parent knew and accepted that growing up was tough on kids these days and they went through awkward phases. They just thought Betty was growing up.

But what Mom and Dad didn't know was what their Betty really got up to after school, where she went, who she met up with, and how science never came into any of it, not in the slightest. They had no idea at all about how their precious Betty had got herself mixed up in some bad, bad activities. Bad news, all of it.

***

Now, this Monday morning, the sun was rising over the tops of the houses and the birds had ceased singing; it was quite late in the eyes of a bird—far too late for the dawn chorus, anyhow. And deep inside number 11, in the purple-painted bedroom right at the back of the house, a large mound stirred and groaned underneath the puffy duvet; lazy, acting-out Betty still lay there in bed and it was edging toward eleven o'clock.

Betty's head with its mop of golden hair—glistering against Betty's illicit eyeliner—peeped out eventually over the top of the duvet. She reached down toward the carpet strewn with its oddments of socks and stockings and sweet wrappers and pulled up her hand in which she held tightly onto her mobile phone. It lit up, a mass of colors.

She pressed the screen, checking her messages. But there was only one; it was her friend Kayla, popping up on WhatsApp.

"Betty-Bet, the bed-head, don't tell me you're in bed *again*?" her friend admonished.

Betty scowled at the screen. "Shut up," she wrote. "You don't know what you're talking about. I'm sick."

"Sick? What d'you mean?" Kayla inquired.

"Sick, like throwing-up kind of sick. Go away," Betty said, rudely. "Can't be bothered messaging." Even her so-called friends got the rough side of Betty's bad moods these days.

"OK," came the reply. And that was that. WhatsApp went quiet.

Betty didn't care.

Nothing much mattered apart from staying in bed and getting a good sleep! She turned over and stuffed her phone under the pillow, falling back to dreamland. She didn't care what Kayla thought, or anyone else for that matter.

But Kayla had made a decision, right there, right then.

It was like a switch had been triggered in her brain.

Okay then; Betty didn't want to chat anymore. So, she would leave lazy, couldn't-care-less, horrible Betty to her own devices.

From now on, Betty was on her own.

And she didn't even know it, because she was asleep. Again.

CHAPTER 3
LITTLE LIES

O n Tuesday evening, Betty's mom and dad had arranged a nice surprise for Betty. Her mom wanted to say thank you to Betty for being so responsible, for looking after herself and the house when they left her alone and went to work.

Betty's mom had bought her some gifts; a handbag Betty had wanted for months and was supposed to be saving up for, some scent and a new skirt to wear after school or on the weekends. It wasn't a short-short skirt of the length Betty loved in secret, but knee-length, boiled wool and expensive.

It was the sort of woollen skirt in which Betty would have looked a million dollars. Because Mom thought Betty was worth it.

Her mom sat on the couch and waited for Betty to come home from classes. It was six o'clock, and Betty's school would have finished long ago—but of course, she had after-school lessons so she should arrive anytime now.

And not only were Mom and Dad waiting for her, but two special visitors had come too, having heard how well Betty was doing at school these days.

Grandma was here, and she'd also bought Betty some-thing out of her pension savings; it was a brand-new, shiny white Apple laptop, something she knew Betty had wanted for a very long time and could never save up for. Betty had been dropping mentions of the amazing MacBook Air—that she really, really needed for school, of course—into just about every conversation, nobody even realizing she knew exactly what she was doing.

And even that was a lie; no kid needed a laptop like that. The school was quite strict about kids not showing up with *flamboyant* or expensive items, since it only made the poorer families suffer and anyway, it made children targets for theft. So, any cast-off computer would do.

But Betty was no fool; she'd always known Grandma would buy her the Apple MacBook eventually. Because that was simply what Grandma did; a little hint dropped surreptitiously into any casual conversation and repeated often enough, and Grandma would think of dipping into her hard-earned pension pot and buying the thing as a gift. Sometimes, she even did it without telling Grandpa. "I put my pension money in the bank," she'd say. "For a rainy day.."

Grandpa would just look at her quizzically, sometimes with his glasses high on his forehead as if he'd worked it all out for himself but was willing to keep a secret. Grandma was way, way too soft.

But Grandma was simply like that; she spent on other people rather than herself, and truth be told, young Betty probably took at least a third of Grandma and Grandpa's total household income. Grandma wasn't very well these days, either; she had osteoarthritis in her hips and knees and getting around was difficult and painful; some days, she even needed a walking frame.

Now, her breathing was getting difficult too, and her heart would miss the occasional beat or go into a strange rhythm. She never mentioned it to anyone, knowing they would tell her to go and get herself back on the heart pills she'd stopped taking, and that it'd cost money she wanted to use for something else, something far more precious.

The $1,000 she had used to buy Betty the Apple laptop could have bought Grandma's medication to make the inflammation of arthritis and the irregular heartbeats all go away. But she would go without caring for her own needs for a few months, just to show Betty how much she was loved and appreciated, and how proud everyone was of her. After all, it was what Grandmas were supposed to do. Nothing, and no one, was as important as Betty.

Betty should have—and always would have—everything she ever wanted, for being such a good and kind girl, devoted to her parents, her studies and her grandma and grandpa.

The time now was seven p.m. There was still no sign of Betty; she was more than an hour late getting home. Mom walked to the window and peeled back the curtains. Grandma looked fractious but said nothing; she knew any of her own words of wisdom would just make it worse and would sound as if she was telling her grown-up daughter quite how to parent Betty.

***

Unfortunately, bad Betty was not even thinking of coming home quite yet. Betty was in a group of older kids, all standing around outside the mall; she was waiting for her new friend Lacey to come out of the stores with some much-needed purchases, especially a pack of cigarettes for Betty.

She knew she was far too young to be smoking but the stress of school was getting to her. Or rather, the stress of not going to school, or playing truant and having to pretend she did attend. Now, Betty was having to tell bigger and bigger lies to cover her errant tracks. This was *real* stress.

A boy called Brett and Betty's friend Lacey came sauntering out of the store, and in the boy's hand, he held the valuable cargo; it was twenty-four smokes, all wrapped in a red and white card pack with a big warning message on the side: SMOKING KILLS.

Sure, Betty thought, *smoking kills, but it won't kill me. It will be a long, long time before I get any problems. Nothing can touch me.*

Betty leaned forward as they approached, holding out her hand.

The kid who had the cigarettes was quite popular in their little friendship group, but he was also the oldest—seventeen—and could be quite mean and manipulative toward the others. It depended on how he was feeling and whether he'd been drinking cider or not. Tonight, he was okay, but still snatched back his arm when Betty held her hand out to receive the cigarettes for which she had already handed over thirty dollars. So, she knew that was way too much for one pack of cigarettes but she also knew there'd be no chance to get back any change.

This boy was trouble, and no way would he give back any money. But she needed him to run her illicit errands.

She held her hand out again. "Brett, come on," she said, her voice weak and faint. "Come on, Brett. Please."

Brett just laughed in her face.

"Give me another twenty, then they're yours," he laughed, taunting her by waving the pack of cigarettes in front of her very nose.

"But that's…"

"Fifty," the boy filled in. "Yeah, fifty dollars in all. And? You got a problem with that, Bett-eee?"

"No," Betty said quietly, fingering her fake nose ring to try and look tougher. But she sure did not feel tough. She felt about seven years old right about now. Betty was suddenly scared to be in this crowd with this boy who was taking advantage of her and stealing all of her money like that.

She wished she could tell her parents.

But then she remembered; this was not her money in the first place, was it? It was her father's. And she had stolen it. For one swift moment—a moment that passed almost before she could realize it—she felt shame. But it passed. She needed, wanted, deserved, this pack of cigarettes. At any cost.

Her pale, shaky hand dipped into her jacket pocket again and pulled out her wallet. She handed over a final crisp twenty-dollar bill. The boy smirked.

Silently, he handed Betty the cigarettes and she cautiously took them, looking as if the very touch of their hands by accident would make her cry. She was not so old and big and tough now, was she?

She looked exactly what she was: she looked like a stupid, foolish, thirteen-year-old now under the influence of some wicked, badly-behaved older kids who'd already chosen to walk along the wrong path in life and who were determined to take her down with them.

She looked small.

She looked like she wanted her mom.

And maybe she did.

Clutching her ill-gotten gains in her trembly right hand, Betty looked down at her wristwatch; it was now ten past seven p.m. and the stores were just about closing up for the night, their squeaky roller shutters coming down and the security guards gradually ushering people toward the mall exit.

Now, she was going to be late home again and breathed a deep sigh, a sigh so big it made her ribs hurt, thinking how angry her mom and dad might be.

"I need to get home," Betty whined to two of the older boys, one of whom had his own car and, she presumed, a driver's license too. He was the boy who had driven the group to the mall. They were miles from home now and Betty had no money left for a cab.

"Not going' back yet," the teenage boy grunted. "I got work to do."

"Work?" Betty asked. Sure, these two boys were old enough for part-time jobs, but she had never heard anyone talk about work before.

"What sort of work?" she asked. She pulled a cigarette out of her pocket and felt around for a lighter.

The two boys laughed loudly, exchanging glances.

"Nothing for a kid to know about!" one said.

It made Betty feel patronized, embarrassed. "Whatever," she mumbled. But it was clear the group had no intention of going back home at all for quite some time. Maybe not for the whole night.

Everyone gathered together again and piled into the boys' two run-down and beaten-up cars. Betty's side of the car didn't even have a seatbelt. Her dad's voice filled her ears:

"Always wear your safety belt, Betty. Your life is very special to your mom and me."

She started to cry but looked out the window so nobody could see; she had to bite her bottom lip till it hurt, to stifle her sobs. All Betty wanted right now was to run home and get straight into bed, where she felt safe.

But she couldn't.

Instead, she pulled out her mobile phone and sent Mom a text. It read:

Hi Mom, Kayla's asked if I can sleep over tonight. Her mom has a headache and can't drive me back.

Of course, this was another lie, but Betty knew her parents would say yes—because they trusted her. And this fact just made Betty feel even worse, but she brushed it aside.

This day was not working out the way Betty had intended.

She had now got herself caught up in a bad, bad crowd and getting away was going to be difficult. More difficult and more costly than a girl like Betty could ever imagine.

***

The next morning, and for the rest of the whole week, Betty's desk and chair at school sat vacant. Vacant as in—no Betty. Nope, not even a sniff of Betty. Not a fragment of Betty! Not a sign of Betty! You get the gist by now.

So, where was Betty? Betty was at her home again, still in bed. One day, she even stayed in bed till three o'clock in the afternoon, only getting up when she knew Mom was due back from work soon.

And in the evenings, Betty made up colorful and entertaining stories for her parents, telling of her fun and educational days at school, how well she'd performed in this and that test, how much she loved school and would make Mom and Dad (and Grandma) so proud!

The family would sit around the dinner table listening in, Mom and Dad's heads nodding away while their smiles beamed ear to ear. But one night, the grins started to fade.

You see, on the Friday evening, things were going to fall apart.

Betty's world full of lies and deception would come undone.

There was a knock at the front door. A loud knock.

Betty was in her room 'doing her homework'—which really meant she was on Facebook again—while Mom was in the kitchen polishing off some chores.

Knock-knock.

Knock-knockety knock!

It was Betty's father who wandered slowly to the door. "Probably the neighbors wanting to borrow something or other," he said to his wife who was drying her hands on a dishcloth.

"What d'you think this time, sweetie? They want to borrow my lawnmower? Ya think they need Betty's help with babysittin' again? They need a lift to—"

Knock, knock, knock, knock.

His words were cut off.

My, things were sure sounding pretty urgent back there at the door. Betty's father hurried up, a little skip in his step. Whenever someone knocked at their door, it usually led to a cheery conversation and maybe a beer or two with an old friend or someone who lived nearby, talking the night away over everything that was wrong in the world, putting it all to rights. He was kinda in the mood for a beer and a good ol' chat right about now.

He grasped the door latch and unfastened the door, pulling it wide.

On the step stood a little woman, someone he didn't recognize. It was a very loud knock for such a diminutive person!

"Mr. Hunniman?" she asked, her squeaking tiny voice reminding him of a mouse—not that he'd ever heard a mouse talk, of course. She hopped from foot to foot, obviously feeling awkward at intruding.

"Yep, that'd be me," he said. "Can I help you at all?"

"Oh, you know, it's probably nothing, but—" She stuck her arm out for a handshake. "I'm Miss Cartmel, from Betty's school. I just wanted to check she was making a recovery and I've brought some get well cards the children made today. We were all so sorry to hear about Betty—you know.".

But Mr. Hunniman didn't know.

He didn't know at all!

That was the very crux of the problem!

Betty's father's eyebrows almost disappeared somewhere around the back of his head. "Um, I'm sorry?" he asked, scratching his ear and then running a hand through his thinning hair.

"Betty's…Betty's, umm, what did you say, again?"

"Betty's recovery, Mr. Hunniman! You know, we were all so sorry to hear she'd been knocked down on the way to school like that. And I'm sure glad she didn't break any bones. Truck drivers these days… should be sued!"

The woman thrust the bundle of cards and small gift-wrapped items over the threshold to Mr. Hunniman.

"Please, I won't take your time but just wanted you to have these. And to know she's okay..." the little plaintive voice came again. "I mean...is she?"

"Oh! Well. Yes, she's—"

The woman smiled.

"Yes," he said. "She's...she's okay."

He looked behind him, stuck for what more to say. Well, what could any man say next after finding out his delightful, diligent daughter, the apple of his eye, had been spinning an intricate web of the most wicked, deceitful lies?

To not show up at school was one thing, but to make up such an evil and appalling, vile story—that was beyond belief! That was something else. Only he wasn't sure what. His brows knitted as he reached out toward the bundle Miss Cartmel held in her tiny little hands.

"Shall I take them out of the carrier bag?" she asked, as if it was important.

"No!" he said, almost yelling. Betty's father was now so anxious and aggrieved, he felt he was about to explode on the spot. Carrier bags? What on earth was the silly woman droning on about? What did carrier bags even matter? Couldn't the woman see his suffering?

He snatched the bag and its contents from the teacher's hands and dropped them on a side table just inside the hallway.

"Sorry," he said, exasperated. "Sorry. I just... well, you know, it's been hard. It's been...well...awful."

The teacher clearly commiserated with the man standing in front of her, having what appeared to be a near nervous breakdown on his own doorstep.

The trauma of his only girl getting almost killed by a rogue truck driver must have been too much to bear. She patted his shoulder lightly. She understood.

"There, there," she said. "I didn't mean to come here upsetting you, Mr. Hunniman. Really, I didn't. I'm so sorry... I just wanted to check on Betty. I hope she gets well soon. So, I'll go. Please give her my—"

"I will!" he said. "I sure will give her yours, and mine too."

The bewildered young teacher backed away slowly and gradually turned around and walked toward the front gate, reaching her hand out to undo the latch. She heard Mr. Hunniman call after her. He was starting to sound a bit weird!

"Oh, yes…you can be sure of it, Miss Cartmel: Betty will be getting better very soon. Sooner than you would have imagined. I'll be making sure of that!"

If Miss Cartmel hadn't known any better, she would have thought he was angry. But she was sure bad news could do that to a man. And she really had no idea of the size of the bad news she had really just dropped upon this usually flawless and problem-free little family.

"Betty!" yelled her father right up the stairs in his loudest voice. "Betty! You get down here right now! I am disgusted to hear what I have just been told."

CHAPTER 4
AFTERMATH

Al that weekend, from Friday night through to Monday morning, Betty cowered in her bedroom, hiding from her parents. She had never seen them so angry, not in her whole life.

They'd spent all of Friday night yelling at Betty, telling her she'd never be anyone or anything, and that she had brought a deep shame upon the whole family, upon hardworking, honest people who only wanted the best for her and who went without things themselves to give her everything she needed.

But it all washed into one ear and out of Betty's other ear.

"Whatever," she'd say. She was quite content hiding away in her room where she could just sleep the days away.

It was what she preferred to do anyhow.

How could that be a punishment?

Stupid parents.

Stupid teachers.

Stupid school.

Stupid everything!

And it was most unfortunate that Grandma had already given Betty the white Apple laptop, and it'd been too late to take it away when her parents finally realized what Betty had really been doing. They had hunted high and low for the Apple MacBook Air—high, low, and every place in between.

They turned over all the furniture in Betty's room and upended her bags and cases, but there was no sign of the $1,000 device anywhere. Instead, they tore Betty's TV connection from the wall and switched off the Wi-Fi router, cutting off all access to the Internet.

It was about all they could do. Meanwhile, Mom had been down to the school and explained how Betty had told a disgusting, dirty, unforgivable lie and how all the lovely, caring kids and teachers had wasted their time and energy worrying for poor Betty who'd supposedly been injured in a road traffic collision. Mom didn't know which way to look.

Mom was deeply, deeply ashamed, even if Betty wasn't.

"I just don't understand it," she wept to the head teacher. "This has never happened to us before. We give Betty *everything*."

The head teacher was empathic but said, slowly and softly, "Well, then, maybe giving a child 'everything' is not what makes them responsible. But don't blame yourself, Mrs. Hunniman. We all make the same mistakes. Even I spoil my children. And you weren't to know. Don't blame yourself, please."

***

Over the coming week, Betty attended school on time but none of the other kids would even talk to her. The teacher must have thought it was the right thing to tell all the rest of the class what she had done.

She thought it was strange she'd received no punishment at school but the fact no one even wanted to know her had been deemed sufficient correction. Betty's behaviour was still the same, though. Now, all the kids of Betty's age were ignoring her, walking away as she approached, turning their backs, *tutting*, whispering when she walked by, pointing fingers and giggling behind their hands. It was still only the older kids who would have anything to do with Betty.

So, she went into school only because the cat was out of the bag and she now had no choice; her own father escorted her to the very door of the school each morning, making himself embarrassingly late for work.

But after school—well, that was another story entirely.

After school, nobody could really make Betty do anything she didn't want to do. They couldn't, could they? Because they weren't there.

After school, Betty would smoke cigarettes, get into the older boys' cars again and go driving around town causing trouble. This was when Betty found out that the 'work' the two older boys—the two who owned their own cars—had mentioned earlier, was that they went stealing small items from the local stores.

And when they had gathered together around stolen $50-worth of goods, they'd go sell their wares to other kids, using the money to buy alcohol and cigarettes—and other things they should not have been having.

It was an exciting way to live and although Betty sometimes felt she was out of her depth, she was now doing so badly at school that she felt she could never catch up anyway, so might as well not try. She was no longer truanting, but she was turning into a horrible monster out of school hours.

Even if Betty had grown horns and breathed fire, she couldn't have been any scarier or more detached from reality.

Her father's voice echoed in her head everywhere she went.

"You'll never make anything of yourself!" and "I'm totally ashamed of you!" And even, "You'll be the death of your poor grandma, you will, Betty!"

They were such ridiculous things to say. Who did he think he was, anyway? What a bully! He had even threatened to take away her mobile phone—but had decided not to because it was Betty's lifeline, her way to call home or for them to reach her if there was an emergency.

But of course, it wouldn't come to that. She just ignored any messaged marked 'Mom' or 'Dad'—sometimes even deleting them unread—and just used the phone for Facebook and social media, and for texting her friends.

And George and Misha next door, or Miriam at the next-door-but-one house, the children Betty used to mix with, were no longer considered her friends; Betty found these kids boring do-gooders with nothing to say for themselves. She now only liked the excitement of the bad kids, the ones who ran wild about the streets causing mayhem for everyone around.

Every day, she came home smelling of cigarettes and she had recently even begun to cuss.

Nobody knew what to do with Betty anymore; she seemed like a lost cause. Only Grandma still had time for Betty these days, once taking her aside to check what was wrong. "Betty, my sweetheart; are you okay? Tell Grandma what's going on in that pretty head of yours."

She had pulled Betty in with an affectionate hug, but Betty had pushed her away. "Grandma, don't," she said, crossly. "I hate when you touch me."

It seemed nobody could do anything right for Betty these days. Not even Grandma. "What you said broke Grandma's heart," Mom had said, but Betty just laughed it off, like she did at everything.

"You can't break someone's heart," she said dismissively, before picking up her warm jacket and disappearing into the night with her friends.

And so, Betty's family members were at their wits' end. They had tried everything, even locking Betty in her room— but she'd only escape through the window. It was now clear it'd take a crisis to sort Betty out.

They hoped one would not come.

But—you guessed it—it did.

CHAPTER 5
FINAL CALL

Today was going to be a problem for Betty. You see, being bad only works for so long, and then things kind of catch up with you. This is the way things are programmed to be. Betty had had a run of good luck where being bad was concerned, but all the bad luck in the world was now about to come chasing after her, and she would find there was no getting away from it no matter where she went. Bad luck was going to come and seek Betty out.

It was Monday morning again, after several weeks of Betty being badly behaved and acting out all the time, whether at home or at school. And on this morning, Betty had actually left her house and her bed at a reasonable hour; the reason was, she was going to play truant with the boys.

Yes, those older boys who were a bad influence on Betty were going to take her to the shopping mall so they could all choose some new outfits—ones they wouldn't pay for, of course. As far as Mom was concerned, though, Betty had gone off to school as usual, since she'd left at exactly the same time as when she was catching the bus. But she didn't catch the bus, did she? No, she didn't. Instead, she stood on the prearranged spot on the street corner, this time waiting for Alfie and Brett to come pick her up out of the line of sight of Mom.

A red car soon rounded the street corner, sounding its horn as it screeched to a halt with the burning of tires and the *pop-pop-bang* of the car exhaust. It left behind a terrible smell and a thick black smoke. If anyone doubted the boys were driving a car unfit to be on the roads, that terrible stink gave it away for sure.

Betty hopped in, but as before, there was no seatbelt. She settled into the backseat with her school bag that was empty, ready for all her stolen gear.

Half an hour later, the three kids arrived at the mall. Betty hopped out and sauntered into the first store on her own. The two boys locked up the run-down vehicle and went into the mall together; they would pick Betty up again later, and Betty would have to give them some of her stolen goods in exchange for the lift each way. Betty started off in a beauty store; she eyed the makeup shelves top to bottom, spying mascara and some lipstick for herself.

She put one lipstick into her hand and raised it up as if taking a good look at it, but as she raised her arm high, she sneakily dropped another into the sleeve of her big jacket where an elasticated cuff kept it in place.

Then she slipped the first one back onto the shelf.

She carried on like this for another few minutes, before deciding that was enough for one store. Her coat sleeve was heavy from all the makeup she had stolen. She headed for the exit.

"Young lady?" a store assistant called as she saw Betty leaving. Betty turned, her face going red all the way down.

"Yes?" she asked. There was no point in running; it just drew more attention to a person and made them look guilty for sure. She stood her ground and turned to face the source of the voice.

"Young lady, you haven't seen nothin' you want to buy today?"

"No, sorry," Betty said. "It's all a bit expensive for me. I only get pocket money," she said. The woman shrugged.

"When you get a bit older, you'll be sure to come back, now."

"Oh," Betty said, smiling. "I will."

She left the store and breathed a sigh of relief. So, no one had seen her stealing stuff after all.

She went to the next store; it was a clothing boutique, harder to steal from, but she had done it before, so—why not? In this store, she saw a blue and white jacket she'd like, so she took it into the changing room with her. Only, she had actually taken the same item twice. In the changing room, she slipped off her jacket and put on the new one, then put her original jacket back over the top, careful to zip it high so the one underneath couldn't be seen.

She nodded to the store girl as she walked past with the identical new jacket over her arm. "Didn't fit me," she said. "But thanks anyway." The attendant smiled at her.

"No problem," she said cheerily.

Betty left the store feeling very smug.

In the third store, she saw a silver-colored watch she liked, on a stand. Mom's birthday was coming up soon and this would be the perfect gift. She pretended to trip over a display stand and knocked it flying. While two store assistants were bending down to retrieve the fallen items, Betty surreptitiously slipped the silvery watch into her pocket. Just like that!

Well, it had been a really successful morning, and she spent a few more hours the same way. Then, at 1 p.m., she walked slowly back to the mall parking garage to meet the boys. She saw Brett's wide grin way before she noticed the car coming back around the corner to pick her up. Brett stood on the sidewalk waiting too. "How'd you get along?" he asked. "Got something for me? I sure hope so."

Betty opened up her bag and showed Brett her collection of stolen items. "Good work," he said, and her head felt as if it would swell with pride. She was good at this. Really good at it. The boys were beginning to ask her to go along.

The car pulled up and the doors were pushed open from the inside. Betty hopped in. The boys started talking.

"That was a near miss, man," one said to the other. "Should've seen the face on that old woman. She was real scared."

They explained to Betty how they'd taken the purse from an elderly lady and knocked her to the ground. Security had chased them, and the medics had to be called to the victim who was clutching at her chest. It made them laugh to recall it and tell their tale. They evidently thought they were two big macho men—both aged seventeen and spotty, with barely enough brains between the two of them to make up half a good one.

Betty's phone was ringing in her bag. As the boys laughed and joked, Betty felt how the phone vibrated relentlessly.

Buzz buzz. Buzz-buzz. BUZZ!

She glanced at the screen inside her bag. It was her father. She silenced the phone and rejected the call.

Ping!

Now, she had a text message.

This was so annoying!

The messages carried on, one after the other.

Finally, she relented and had a look. The car kept on moving toward its destination where the goodies were all supposed to get shared out, but now, Betty was banging on the back of the driver's seat.

"Stop! I need to get out. Stop! Please!"

She was white in the face and looked queasy.

"Shut up, stupid girl," one boy said, looking behind him at her.

"Please, stop, it's… I had bad news. It's…it's real bad… Please!" She started to cry, and her voice cracked. All they could hear was Betty's wailing from the back seat. They stopped, not wanting to listen to this noise.

"Get out then, stupid."

"But you owe us for the lift," the other one reminded her.

One of the boys walked around to Betty's side of the car and tugged her out roughly, by her jacket sleeve. She was sent sprawling on the sidewalk, crying.

She ran, ran, ran, as fast as her legs would carry her, back toward home. Luckily, there wasn't far to go. She tried to call home as she ran, but she was crying too much to speak.

***

Betty hurtled into her house through the side door, to see her mother and father in an embrace in the kitchen.

"What happened to Grandma?" Betty cried, her black mascara flooding down the side of her face. The text messages had told Betty that Grandma had been taken to hospital and might not make it.

It was clear Mom and Dad had both been crying.

Betty now cried so hard too; she thought she would never stop.

She cried thinking of all the lovely things Grandma had done for her, even when Betty was bad, even when she was rude, and even when she was thoughtless, dismissive and ungrateful.

"Grandma was knocked to the ground in the mall," Mom said, weeping. "There were some…boys. Nasty, horrible boys. They knocked your Gran to the ground and took her money. It was all she had left. And she hit her head on the floor, and…and her heart's gone. She had a heart attack, they think."

Mom burst into tears. Betty ran forward and hugged her; they cried on each other. Father sat with his head in his hands, occasionally blowing his nose on a vast cloth handkerchief.

"What's happening to our young people?" he said. His voice was shaky too. Betty had never seen her parents in such a state. Dad turned to Betty now, as if she would know the answer.

"Betty," he said, softly. "You tell me. What did Grandma do to anyone?"

"Mom, Dad, please don't cry!" Betty said, "Because it's more than I can stand. Grandma will be… Grandma… will be okay," she sobbed. "Grandma has to be okay. The hospital will make her better. They have to."

"It's not that easy, sweetheart," Betty's father cried. He had big tears sliding down his face. "She needs a lot of treatment now, baby girl, and she needs x-rays and scans and all sorts. And then there's the heart problem because we didn't know she wasn't paying for her heart medication any-more…and she'd even stopped paying for her health insur-ance."

Betty's heart sank. Her blood ran cold in her veins.

"Her…h…heart treatment?"

"Yes, your Grandma had a bad heart, you know? But she stopped paying for her repeat medications a few months ago… she said she was saving up for something. A thousand dollars…"

Betty ran to the bathroom and threw up. Tears stung her eyes.

A thousand dollars?

Her knees wobbled.

Grandma… Grandma had saved exactly that amount for Betty's Apple MacBook Air, that computer Betty had gone on and on about until finally, Grandma had softened and offered to buy it, thinking it was essential for Betty's schoolwork. But it was not essential at all. Betty wanted it. Needed it. To sell… so she could buy cigarettes and clothes.

That was why Mom and Dad could not find the laptop when they'd wanted to punish Betty by taking it away. But Mom and Dad had never realized it was new and had cost so much, because Grandma had kept it a secret.

Betty could hardly speak. She thought of Grandma saving all of her pension money to buy something for which Betty hadn't even been grateful, and she thought of how Grandma had put her own life on the line to make it happen for Betty. Then Betty had just got rid of the laptop. For what? $100, as far as she could recall. And the $100 were gone in the blink of an eye. Just like the $100 cash she had stolen from her own father.

And now things got even worse, because Dad reached into his wallet to see how much money he could put toward Grandma's treatment. But the wallet was empty. "I—I don't understand," he said, scratching his head. But Betty understood, because only the night before, she had been tempted by the cash and had taken it. Luckily, she still had it in her room.

"Mom," she whispered to her mother as she slipped the crumpled ten-dollar bills into her mom's hand, "I'm so sorry. I am so horrible. This is Dad's money."

Her mother looked at Betty, her mouth agape, her eyes wide. "Oh, Betty…" she said. Mom's face was filled with disappointment. "Oh, Betty…" And then she broke down in tears. "Betty," she whimpered, "You are a horrible, horrible child. And you cannot come with us to see Grandma. You do not deserve to see Grandma ever again. And you do realize, Betty, even if she makes it—she might never, ever forgive you."

The words were harsh. The words were deserved, Betty knew that. But the words made Betty feel as if she was nothing, a nobody, a girl so ugly and awful and cruel that she did not deserve to see her own grandmother again.

Now, Betty's head was a whirlwind of all the terrible things she had done, all within the last few weeks. She thought of how all this acting out had led to Grandma's life being placed at risk.

She hated herself. She hated those boys. She hated what she had turned into. Now, she had nothing left of value; even Mom and Dad hated her.

Mom and Dad had no words to say to bad Betty; they shook their heads with tear-filled eyes, and left the house, starting up the car. They headed for the hospital with every penny they could get together between them. Betty's father had been so angry, he'd just walked into Betty's room and snatched back up the $20 bill he had just left there for Betty's pocket money before she'd come home. And Betty saw him do it, but she had nothing to say.

There was nothing she *could* say.

She cried and hung her head in shame.

"I'm sorry," she wept, but the house was empty now and there was no one to hear her. "I'm sorry, I'm sorry, I'm sorry…" She howled like an injured puppy for a whole hour, wondering what would become of Grandma.

The evening became the night. It stretched on and on, and on, each second seeming to last an hour, Betty lying there all alone atop her cold bed, lost, wondering, hoping.

The stars came out and twinkled down at her from the black sky. She looked up from her bed through the open curtains and cried, and cried, and cried. She wondered if Grandma would make it. She hoped so. She really, really hoped so. She tried to look for signs in the stars and sky, but there were none.

If Grandma made it through, Betty knew she would never, ever be naughty again. She wouldn't act out, she wouldn't skip school, and she would be a model pupil in every lesson. And she would make her grandma proud. She would pass all her exams and she would decide on a college to go to, where she would get a degree. And her grandma would be the guest of honor and her grandma would say, "I knew you would make it, my beautiful Betty! Well done, my Betty!"

"I'm sorry, Grandma," she whispered among all her tears now, as they dripped off her cheeks and her nose. "I love you so, so much, Grandma. Please get better. I love you. I'm sorry, I'm sorry, I'm sorry…I'm…sorry."

Her pillow was soaked with tears.

And at 9 p.m., when Mom and Dad still had not come home, Betty curled up tight on her bed and tried to cry herself to sleep. But, too tired to undress and get underneath her duvet, she pulled her big black jacket around her. It stank of cigarettes. She reached into the pockets and pulled out all the unused packs. One by one, she pulled the cigarettes from their boxes and put them in a small pile. Then she walked to the bathroom and flushed every single one down the toilet.

She returned to her bedroom and sat on the edge of the bed, sending God a silent and heartfelt prayer for her wonderful Grandma. Then she lay down once more and drifted off into a deep sleep.

In Betty's sleep, a dream came to her. In the dream, God had been having trouble sleeping that night, and He had got up to make Himself a cup of tea! Then He had heard Betty crying and listened to her emotional prayer.

God walked to Betty's bedside and gently stroked her wet hair off her face, where it was stuck down with tears. She was fast asleep. But God did not care if she was asleep or awake. "You are still my child," He whispered. "My children are everywhere, and they are in all shapes and sizes. Some are good, and some are cruel and bad, like you, Betty. I do not care that you are bad… I will always love you and watch over you."

God rested a hand on Betty's forehead and left it there a minute, in silence. "Betty, Grandma will be fine. The goodness in you will see that she is. And the goodness in me will see that you look after Grandma."

And with that, Betty's dream died away, and she slept a restful sleep for eight hours straight. In the early hours of the morning, she woke and noticed her parents' car was back in their driveway and they had gone to sleep in their bed. She would not wake them, as desperate as she was to know how

Grandma's night had been. She would learn to wait for all of the things she wanted.

She was still tearful and afraid—but something in Betty told her that Grandma would make it.

Grandma would be fine, and all would be well with the world.

And she knew, somehow, that it was her own job to make sure of it.

Betty felt strangely at peace with the world, and with herself.

CHAPTER 6
BETTY'S BEGINNING

Weeks had passed. Betty's grandma had recovered and was back at her own home, but Betty had still not seen her. She felt frightened, embarrassed and ashamed of the evil girl she had been, of how she had let herself be led astray by the wrong crowd of kids, and of how mean and selfishly she'd behaved.

Betty's mom and dad were always going to see Grandma, but Betty would always wring her hands and hope they would ask her to come along.

But they didn't ask her to go along with them, and she didn't feel she deserved to mention it. They just left her at home with a neighbour watching over her, telling her to be good. She would just nod sadly and silently. Her heart broke at not being able to see Grandma. But she didn't know what Grandma would say or do even if she did see her. Maybe seeing Betty would be too much for Grandma's weak heart. Grandma must surely hate her.

Now, everyone knew Betty was the friend of those boys who had caused Grandma's fall and stolen her money. Everyone also knew Betty was the one who'd sold the laptop

Grandma had given Betty, the laptop bought with money Grandma couldn't even afford. And Betty was the one who'd stolen from Dad's wallet too. The shame of it all would never go. It was going to be like a black dog always on Betty's heels. But now, there was one good thing.

The good thing was that something had changed; Betty remembered the dream in which God had got up in the night to make a cup of tea and in which he had taken care of her. Of course, in real life, even Betty knew God was not a person and God would not be roaming around the kitchen making tea late at night! Or would He?

Who was she to know these things?

Maybe God even munched all the cookies that seemed to go missing!

And besides, it was reassuring to think God was there.

A small part of Betty believed everything would be fine since God was still at her side and watching over everything she did. Betty now believed if she was patient and stayed away from trouble, good things would come.

So, Betty went to school like never before. She was early at her lessons and always did her homework without being reminded. She put all of her energy and effort into her studies, and in her spare time, she wrote short stories and entered competitions. Betty was a good writer, and like many kids who had travelled down the wrong path before finding the right way to go, her experiences had only made her creative writing even better. Betty had a lot to say for herself.

The one thing Betty could not shake off was the guilt—the guilt over Grandma's $1,000. It was because Grandma hadn't taken her heart medication—

because she had stopped paying for it in order to fund Betty's Apple MacBook—

that Grandma's old heart had had 'a funny turn' that day in the mall after the boys attacked her. And until Grandma started taking the medication again, she was at risk of another bad episode.

***

More weeks passed. Betty was doing so well at school that Mom and Dad had been called in to the head teacher's office to hear that all the teachers were full of praise for Betty. She had totally turned around her behaviour and her life.

And even better; Grandma was coming to tea. She had decided to come and see Betty, as painful as it all was for both of them.

Betty was scared but she was also excited. This was her chance to put everything right between them.

That evening, when Grandma arrived, Betty was sitting on the couch, swinging her legs, her eyes threatening to well with tears. But as soon as the door swung open and Grandma came in, Betty ran to her and almost knocked the old woman off her feet a second time. The pair hugged tightly and cried in silence. They were both afraid to be the first one to speak.

But Betty was fourteen now; she was growing into a young woman and she was determined to take responsibility for everything, and to hide from nothing. So, eventually, she looked Grandma in her eyes and whispered, "I am so sorry, Grandma. I was so scared I had lost you—and that it'd be all my fault."

"Betty, sweetheart," the old woman said, "It was my fault, that stupidity with the laptop. I was a silly old fool, wanting you to have everything even when it cost me my health. I can't hold you responsible for that!"

They hugged tighter.

"But those boys, Nana," Betty said, "*They* were my fault."

She expected her grandma to say no, they weren't.

"If you say so," Grandma said. "If you say so."

They hugged even tighter and Grandma could feel Betty's whole body shaking.

"But have you learned your lesson, Betty? Will you be better now?"

"Grandma, I will never go there again. I am already better. I will show you... I am so sorry, Grandma, and I love you so much. I couldn't live with myself if—" Betty burst into tears. "I love you so much. I'm so sorry. I'm so sorry..." Tears streamed down Betty's pink cheeks.

"Shh," Grandma said. "It is all done now, it's all past. Your grandma is too old to even remember such garbage! Look, I can barely remember what happened yesterday!" They both laughed through tears. "And anyway, today is Betty's new beginning. That's all we have to worry about. Only that."

Betty had no words.

She just nodded and hugged Grandma with all her strength.

Grandma stayed in their house that night, taking the small single room next to Mom and Dad. Grandma took off her clothes, pulled on her flowery nightgown and slipped into bed. Something peculiar crinkled between the sheets.

Grandma was perplexed. What on earth was this strange and lumpy, papery thing in the bed? She reached in and pulled out a fat envelope.

Scrawled on it, in Betty's handwriting in black pen, with a red love heart after Grandma's name, it said, *Grandma's Healthcare Fund*.

Grandma opened it with a shaky hand. Her heart was full of love, and the envelope full of cash. It came to $1,500! Wrapped around all the bills was a paper certificate that Grandma read aloud: *To: Betty Hunniman, in recognition of the Best Submission, American Young Teens Short Story Competition. 1ˢᵗ Prize $1,500.* "Oh! My clever, clever girl!" Grandma said to herself. "I knew you could do it!" But the cash wasn't all that was in the envelope. A tiny torn-off slip of paper in Betty's handwriting said, *For you, for always, with all my love from your Better Betty (and God).*

Grandma chuckled and chuckled again. She laughed until her belly started to hurt. 'And God?' Wherever did the child get such a crazy idea?

EPILOGUE

Four years later:

Betty Hunniman was a brand-new girl now. It was as if she had been reborn with a beautiful soul and good intentions. She had grown up; almost losing someone so precious had been a special lesson, one she appreciated and would never forget.

Now, Betty had turned eighteen. She was a young woman, full of life and enthusiasm for what she loved to do. And what was it that Betty truly loved to do, you ask? Betty had begun training on a course in social work, specializing in troubled teens. She still loved social media and Facebook, so she'd put that to good use too.

She had passed all her exams with flying colors and she discovered hidden talents she'd never known she had. Such as using her social media skills to raise funds, setting up a drop-in center for teens who were getting into trouble just as she had been only five years earlier.

Young Betty was now recognized as one of the town's successful young entrepreneurs, and people came from all over the state to speak to Betty about their teens' problems. Kids who were in trouble with the law, kids playing truant from school, kids who bullied their siblings and disobeyed their parents and their teachers were all coming to Betty from far and wide.

She was a teen guru! And what's more, she never kept secret her fall from grace and how she had almost caused the loss of her own grandma. In fact, Betty told this story to help other kids see how well she had done. If Betty could stoop so low and yet get back on her feet, they could too.

She equipped her drop-in center to provide experts offering counseling and therapy, to give kids a listening ear, and to offer a place where teens would always have a friend and a mentor. And more than that; she made sure all the staff and volunteers like her mother and grandmother had plenty of affection and love to offer.

Now, Betty was winning awards, giving talks, opening day-care centers, visiting schools and colleges—inspiring kids just like her to be bigger, better, braver. Braver, yes, because they would learn how to say no to the bad things, and how to say yes only to the good things. And she called her center *The Better Transit*. It was a name everyone knew, and everyone loved.

And one afternoon, the drop-in center was welcoming four new volunteers. When they all walked in, Betty could not believe her eyes! In came George and Misha, her old neighbors who had once lived next door! She squealed loudly in excitement. "George! Misha! I knew you'd come!"

And there, too, was Betty's ex-best friend, Kayla. She hadn't seen Kayla for years! They'd not spoken ever since Betty had told Kayla to go away. But now, it was like the friends had never been apart. They hugged so tightly.

Then the fourth volunteer came in. Sure, this one was a little slow on her feet and she looked a little crooked and frail, but enthusiasm and mischief glowed in her pale blue eyes.

"Room for a little one in your kitchen?" Grandma asked.

She already had her best apron on, ready to do chores. She was on her new heart medication and brim full of energy. "You're the boss, young Betty," she said. "Tell us all what to do. C'mon, let's go, no time for standing around!"

"Grandma!" Betty cried. "I definitely have room for a little one! How about you go make tea? God will help you. He's in the back, waiting. But keep him out of the cookie jar."

Everyone laughed.

SUMMARY

Betty had to be the laziest being in the entire universe.

Every kid in Cherry Avenue knew it. All the teachers in their local school could swear by it. But she didn't care. Her nicknames weren't "Lazy Betty" and "Bone-idle Betty" among other similar names for nothing. She had to live up to the hype.

But that wasn't the worst of it.

Betty was a chronic liar, a thief and an unrepentant truant. But her delinquency was about to catch up with her in the most unexpected and unpleasant of ways, and she would never remain the same again.

A Better Betty is a poignant story that draws attention to juvenile truancy in the 21st century Generation Z teenager. It points out the dangers of the modern tendency of parents to leave their kids unsupervised due to the pressures of a demanding career.

C. Pierre-Russell

C. Pierre-Russell was born and raised in sunny Miami, FL, it was natural for Cheurlie Pierre-Russell to join the United States Navy.

Her high point came during Operation Uphold Democracy on the island nation of Haiti, where she worked as a translator. Leaving the Navy was difficult but it was time to start a family and tackle a new career.

C. Pierre-Russell graduated from Georgia State University with a Bachelor of Arts in Sociology, later earning a Master of Science in Psychology from Walden University.

Her desire to strive in education led her to study the development and perception of children's lives through the influence of social context, and she has also studied children's intellectual development.

These combined areas of interest influenced her to write children's books, to help them understand their own cognitive way of life.

A strong role model for women and children, C. Pierre-Russell is a wife and has three amazing children of her own.

Now, she writes both fiction and non-fiction for kids of all ages, covering many subjects.

C. Pierre-Russell feels every child is a future leader and deserves only the best!

To find out about C. Pierre-Russell's next book release, visit her Instagram page: https://www.instagram.com/j3russellbook/ or her Facebook page: https://www.facebook.com/russellbook